The Story of Robin Hood

Illustrated by Alan Marks

Retold by Rob Lloyd Jones

It was a quiet night in Sherwood village.

Yet someone was creeping through the dark...

From his bedroom window, Jack Fletcher watched the shadowy figure flit from roof to roof.

"It's Robin Hood," he whispered.

Jack longed to meet Robin Hood – the famous outlaw who robbed from the rich to give to the poor.

That night, Robin Hood left purses by the villagers' doors, filled with glittering golden coins.

But the very next day, the Sheriff of Nottingham rode into the village.

"Give me your money," he barked.
"Or I'll have you all arrested."

The King was overseas, so now the Sheriff thought
he could do whatever he pleased.

Jack hated the Sheriff of Nottingham. When no one was looking, he scooped up some horse dung... ...and hurled it **SPLAT** in his face.

The Sheriff went red with rage. "Arrest that boy!" he spluttered.

"Run, Jack!" his father cried.

Jack fled into Sherwood Forest.
His heart was pounding and
tears trickled down his cheeks.

From the safety of the forest, Jack saw
soldiers dragging his father away.

He was being arrested,
and it was all Jack's fault.

Branches creaked and groaned as Jack
stumbled deeper into the forest.

Ahead, a lone rider appeared
between the tangled trees.

Jack recognized her at once. It was Lady Marian, the King's cousin. "I'm lost," Jack sobbed. "And my father's been arrested..."

Marian smiled at him. "Don't worry," she said, "I know someone who can help."

They rode to a clearing in the forest, with a circle of huts around a crackling fire. "What is this place?" Jack asked.

"It's our hideout," a voice called.

Four outlaws hid among the trees. "I'm Will Scarlet," said the first, sitting on a branch.

"I'm Little John," said another, rubbing his bushy red beard.

Friar Tuck

Little John

"And my name's Friar Tuck," said the third, with a cheery wave.

Will Scarlet

Jack already knew who the fourth man was.

"Robin Hood!" he gasped. "Will you help me rescue my father?"

Robin Hood

Robin led Jack back to the village.

"Your father is held deep inside the Sheriff's castle," he said.
"And the castle is a dangerous place. We must wait
until the time is right to rescue him."

So Jack learned to live
like an outlaw.

He robbed from the rich...

...and gave to the poor.

Robin's gang taught him how to
fight with a sword...

...and he learned to fire arrows with skill and speed.

Jack loved being part of Robin's gang, but he couldn't forget his father, locked up in the Sheriff's castle.

One day, while Robin and Jack were alone in the hideout, Marian came charging up.

"The village is on fire!" she cried.

The villagers wandered among the smoky ruins. "It was the Sheriff's soldiers," they told Robin. "They captured the rest of your gang."

"It's time to fight back," Robin declared, flourishing his sword.

In the dead of night, Robin and Jack snuck up
to the Sheriff's castle.

They dropped onto the moonlit wall.
Everything was eerily quiet.

Suddenly, a door burst open. Guards lunged at Robin, whirling their swords. Steel blades clashed and clanged.

Robin twisted and twirled, driving the guards back into the castle.

But there were too many guards, with too many swords.
"I've got you now," snarled the Sheriff of Nottingham.

Just then, the castle gate flew open.
Marian and the villagers stormed inside.

"Charge!" they shouted,
and a fierce battle began.

Jack and Marian raced down to the castle dungeon
to free the prisoners.

"Father!" Jack cried.

Jack's father scooped him up in a big hug.
"Hooray for Jack!" the prisoners cheered. "He's saved us all."

But the fight wasn't over yet. Back in the hall,
the Sheriff refused to surrender.

"*You* can't stop me," he growled.

"No," boomed a voice from the castle entrance, "but *I* can..."

"You're back!" Marian cried, as the King strode into the castle.

The Sheriff's sword clattered to the ground.

He tried to run away, but Jack tripped him up and he tumbled headlong into the dark dungeon.

Silently, Robin and his gang slipped away
into Sherwood Forest.

"Robin Hood!" Jack called. "Will I ever see you again?"

"You will," the outlaw replied, "whenever you need me."

Edited by Lesley Sims & Susanna Davidson

Designed by Louise Flutter

Digital manipulation: John Russell

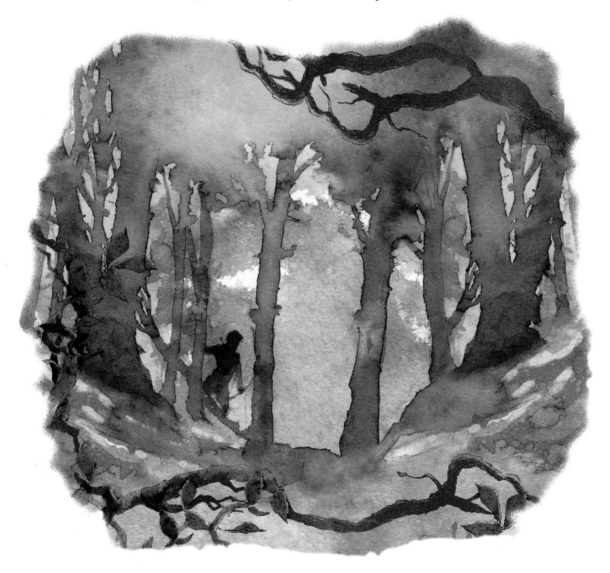